Shiva and Nandi the Bull

Shubha Vilas

Om Books International

Once there was a virtuous sage named Shilada. He was very unhappy because he did not have a child he could love. His well-wishers advised him to pray to Indra and please him. Shilada liked the idea. Only Indra, the king of heaven could grant him the child he desired.

So Shilada set off to the mountains with hope in his heart that when he came back, he would be a happy man, blessed with a son.

After a few years of austerities, Indradeva was pleased with Shilada and appeared before him. Shilada was overjoyed when he saw Indra standing before him. When Indra asked him the reason for his penance, Shilada revealed his heart's desire.

‘Please give me a son who is not born from a mother, lives forever, and is equal to Lord Shiva.’

Indra, who had been smiling till now, suddenly became grave. ‘Only Lord Shiva can help you,’ he replied, ‘please pray to him.’

Very disappointed, Shilada continued his intense meditation. Hundreds of years passed. He was determined that he would not stop meditating till Lord Shiva himself appeared before him.

He had stopped eating and drinking. His body had shrunk. He was now only a bag of bones. Ants and termites took him to be a rock, so they started building their homes inside his body. Shilada was covered with anthills. Insects were nibbling on his bones. Yet, his mind was absorbed in Shiva.

Finally, the vibes of Shilada's prayers reached Lord Shiva in Kailash. He immediately appeared before his devotee. Lord Shiva touched him on his head. Shilada felt a thrill of energy run through his body. His wounds healed. His flesh and muscles gained vigour once again. He sprang up and offered his obeisance to his Lord.

No words were needed as Shiva encouraged him to speak. Shilada's words gushed out from his mouth, in anticipation of the boon.

'My Lord, please bless me with a child who is not born from a mother, and who lives eternally.'

'As you wish,' said Shiva, 'you may go back home and perform a yagya that will give you a child.'

Saying this, Shiva disappeared in a flash, leaving Shilada dazed. Once he came to his senses, Shilada hurried home to perform the yagya.

Out of the sacrificial fire emerged a strong, young lad clad with dazzling diamonds. How delighted Shilada was to see his dream come true! He named the boy Nandi, meaning one who is forever happy.

Shilada took Nandi home. Nandi was now transformed into a normal boy. His dazzling aura had gone. No one could guess how extraordinary his birth had been. Nandi became an ardent devotee of Shiva.

Shilada began his education by teaching him from the scriptures. Nandi was now ready to start his learning from a guru.

When he met the guru, Shilada was shocked to hear his words. He prophesied that Nandi had only one more year to live.

Once again, Shilada was pushed into a world of sorrow. Unable to see his father's pain, Nandi went to the Himalayas to appease Lord Shiva. Shiva appeared and revealed the truth to him, 'Dear Nandi, you were originally in Kailash and were cursed by a muni to take human birth. It is now time for you to leave your human body and come back to your eternal spiritual form. You will always remain in my service and the world will pray to you first, before entering my temple.'

Nandi then transformed himself into half-human and half-bull to serve Lord Shiva. He is the guardian and vehicle of Lord Shiva and devotees pray to him for permission to visit Lord Shiva.